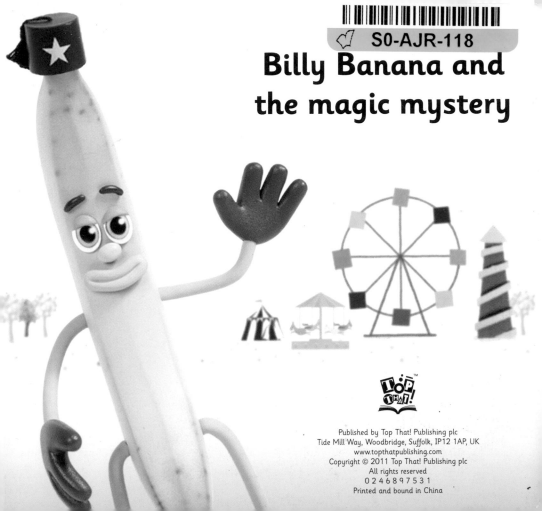

Billy Banana and the magic mystery

Published by Top That! Publishing plc
Tide Mill Way, Woodbridge, Suffolk, IP12 1AP, UK
www.topthatpublishing.com
Copyright © 2011 Top That! Publishing plc
All rights reserved
0 2 4 6 8 9 7 5 3 1
Printed and bound in China

What scene have the
children made today?

A fairground ...

One day, Billy Banana stepped into the children's playscene. The children had created a fairground.

Billy loves magic tricks and when they go well, he is a brilliant magician. But, most of the time, his magic tricks go very, very wrong!

Looking around at the fairground rides and big tents, Billy decided that he would put on an amazing magic show for his Frooble friends that afternoon.

'I must rehearse my show,' Billy thought.
'I want my tricks to be perfect!'

So, Billy held up his magic bag, pretending to show the audience that it was empty.

'Abracadabra,' he chanted. 'My magic power will fill the bag with a pretty flower!'

Billy rummaged in his magic bag and held up … a playing card!

'That's not right!' he gasped.

Billy put the card away and decided to try again.

'With magic powers,' he chanted, 'it shouldn't be hard to conjure up a playing card!'

With a flourish, Billy held up ... a line of flags!

'That's not right either,' he groaned.

Practising the trick for a third time, Billy took a deep breath and chanted, 'Alley-kazam, alley-kazee, a line of flags we'd like to see!'

Feeling around his magic bag, Billy held up ... a flower!

'Another wrong trick!' he wailed.

By now, it was nearly time for the show to begin and Billy's friends would be arriving very soon.

'What am I going to do?' gulped Billy. 'I still haven't perfected my tricks!'

Billy put down his magic bag and sighed. Then, he saw Sienna Strawberry running towards him. She looked very worried.

'Billy, you have to help me! I went on the ferris wheel with Bobby Blackberry and lost him in the crowd afterwards. Now I can't find him anywhere!'

By now, the other Froobles had arrived for Billy's show. However, when they heard that Bobby had gone missing, they all set off in search of him.

'I might as well join them,' thought Billy.

After a while, everyone returned with disappointed looks on their faces.

'There's no sign of Bobby,' sighed Sienna.

'I looked by the rollercoaster and the helter-skelter,' added Orlando Orange.

'I even checked inside the haunted house!' shuddered Tessa Tomato.

Suddenly, Billy's magic bag moved!

'Did you see that?' gasped Orlando, pointing in amazement.

Everyone gathered round, watching and waiting.

'There! It moved again!' exclaimed Tessa.

'How is it moving?' asked Orlando.
'It must be Billy's magic!'

Everyone began to clap and cheer.

'This is the best magic show we've ever seen!' they all agreed.

But, Billy knew that it wasn't one of his magic tricks. So he hurried over and peeked into the bag.

'I'll show you how the bag is moving,' Billy chuckled. 'Bobby curled up inside to have a nap!'

Everyone was thrilled to have found Bobby, and they crowded round to watch Billy perform the tricks that he had practised earlier ... and this time he got them all right!

Billy had learnt that if at first you don't succeed, try, try again ... even if things don't turn out quite as you would expect!